Flooty Hobbs

and the Jiggling, Jolly Gollywobber

Story by
J. W. Dixon and Jem Sullivan

Illustrations by
Jem Sullivan

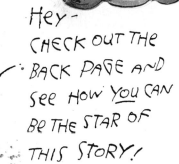

Here is a story about

Christopher Mann,

the Kid who wasn't afraid!

Hey —
CHECK OUT THE
BACK PAGE AND
SEE HOW *YOU* CAN
BE THE STAR OF
THIS STORY!

This book was made

especially for

Christopher Mann

With love from

Mommy and Pappy

April 3, 1994

Christopher Mann
The kid who wasn't afraid.

I thought everyone
was scared of me...

until I met Christopher Mann, age 6.
Now I'll never be the same.

It was a night like any other.

Christopher Mann
6741-6 McClellan
Fort Riley, Kansas

As always,
I waited
through the usual
bedtime routine.

First, the
pajamas...

Then, teeth
were brushed...

Christopher

Faces were washed.

At last, the bedtime story was told.

The
End.

The ZOO is BLUE
...and there's the Read!
James W. Dixon

The lights went out, and it was
finally time to appear. But
I didn't know that Christopher
had a plan.

Here's what happened.

My scary friends and I approached the bed.
As usual, I got to go first.
I made my scariest face...

but all I heard from underneath the covers
was "Tee hee, tee hee. You don't scare me!"

That's when Spooky Luke spoke up.
"You call that scary, Flooty? Let me try!"
he insisted.

He got the same response.

Tee Hee, Tee Hee.
You DON'T SCARE ME!

Scary Larry was next. "Nice try, Luke.
Now step aside. Here's a new face I've
been working on. This will be *real*
scary."

Christopher's Bed

But he got the same response, too.

One by one, we all took turns making our scariest faces. And one by one...

It had always been so simple. But tonight Christopher was not so easy to scare.

So, we decided to all make faces together on the count of three.

This time, from underneath the covers,
there was *no* reply.

Complete silence.

We blinked in the darkness.

Straining to hear,
I leaned closer.

Then we all leaned closer...

and closer still...

ALLOW ME TO introduce myself.
I'm Flooty Hobbs.
Maybe you know me...
Maybe you don't.

Everybody shrieked,
shrank and scattered,
except for me.
I was too scared
to move. So I just
stood and trembled.

Who could blame me?!
Everybody knows that a
Gollywobber (especially a jolly
one that jiggles) is the one
thing that can strike terror
into the heart of any bedtime
monster. And that includes
me, Flooty Hobbs.

"You don't have to be afraid," said the Gollywobber. "I'm really Christopher Mann."

"If you look closer, you'll see
I'm just pretending to
be a Gollywobber.

33

And I can see that
you and your friends are
nothing more than shadows in the dark.
That's nothing to be afraid of."

With that,
I knew I would never be
looked at the same, so
I had to leave, never to return.

The last thing I heard Christopher
say, snuggling back under the covers
was "Tee hee tee hee. You'll never
scare me."

and you know, the kid was right.